John Richard Barlow

John's Trip or a Visit to Niagara

A Serio-Comic Poem in Four Cantos

John Richard Barlow

John's Trip or a Visit to Niagara
A Serio-Comic Poem in Four Cantos

ISBN/EAN: 9783337145002

Printed in Europe, USA, Canada, Australia, Japan

Cover: Foto ©Andreas Hilbeck / pixelio.de

More available books at **www.hansebooks.com**

JOHN'S TRIP,

OR

A Visit to Niagara.

A SERIO-COMIC POEM,

IN FOUR CANTOS,

BY

JOHN R. BARLOW,

AUTHOR OF THE "MAIDEN OF THE MIST," &C.

NIAGARA FALLS:

WILLIAM POOL, PRINTER,

GAZETTE BUILDING.

———

1871.

JOHN'S TRIP,

OR

A VISIT TO NIAGARA.

CANTO I.

I want a hero: an uncommon want,
　When every year and month sends forth a new one;
Till, after cloying the gazettes with cant,
　The age discovers he is not the true one;
Of such as these I should not care to vaunt,
　I'll therefore take our ancient friend Don Juan!

　　　　　　　　　　　　　—BYRON.

Aspiring genius, fiery youth!
　Oh! thoughts and feelings great,
Which lead us on to deeds that seem,
　Scarce pre-ordained by fate.
Oh! how we long for something more,
　Than that which heav'n has sent,
And vainly strive for empty joys,
　Till fire of youth is spent.

But pray, begone, ye puerile thoughts
　Of sentimental strain;
The joys of youth we cherish dear,
　For they are not in vain;
They fill the heart with lightsome scenes,
　Redeeming us from care;
They cheer us down the vale of life,
　With retrospection rare.

Bright dreams of what may sometimes be—
  But "castles in the air,"—
Though ye full often disappoint,
  Ye are of life a share!
Ye lead us on to deeds, which may
  By age be sore condemned;
But who, in youthful years, e'er thought
  Of what might be the end!

Thus thought a youth, who long had lived
  A life of happy dreams;
Whose dearest wish was that, sometime,
  He'd bask in Fortune's beams;
Long had he dwelt, contented, in
  His eastern country home,
Till youthful aspirations taught
  His heart a wish to roam.

But here, unto his youthful mind,
  A question did arise,
Where he would go, that he might see
  The most to cause surprise;
And having read and heard folks say
  Niagara was not slow,
Made up his mind, without delay,
  To that place he would go.

Then all was hurry, rush and haste,
  And time most precious grew ;
One meagre week was all he had,
  In which to see it through ;
He packed his carpet-bag with speed,
  His wardrobe on his back ;
And from his friends, he then received
  Of good advice, no lack.

And feeling, like a prudent youth,
  That life is but a breath,
He bought a ticket, to ensure
  His friends, in case of death ,
Though there are some, without a doubt,
  Who'd think it little loss,
If he by fate, or circumstance,
  Should chance to get a toss.

But hoping that he'll have good speed,
  And come back, safe and sound,
We beg his leave to fellow him
  Upon his journey round ;
To tell what he may hear, and see,
  And feel, and think and say ;
To set it down, in mirthful strain,
  As jottings by the way.

Then first and foremost, to begin,
　　Our hero—yes, 'tis so—
A tale without a hero would
　　Be worthless as you know.—
What matter, though he chance to be
　　A youth of humble birth!
Who knows, but he in time to come
　　May prove a man of worth!

The days of bold Knight Errantry,
　　Have long since passed away;
And heroes, now, are chosen from
　　Men of the present day,
And how much nobler in this land,
　　Where poverty's no ban,
To feel, when years have left us gray,
　　We stand a "self-made man!"

And now our Hero with a name,
　　We shall proceed to grace,
By which, to us, he may be known
　　Through change of time and place;
We'll call him John—an honest name,
　　As always has been shown;
I like it, too—perchance, because
　　It proves to be my own.

But if my mem'ry serves me right,
  I planned myself, to tell
That which our Hero heard and saw,
  And what to him befell.
The first thing then, the which he saw,
  With selfishness replete,
Was how each one, for self inclined,
  Strove for a double seat.

And, being of an aptish turn,
  And ripe for learning fast,
He thought he'd serve himself the same,
  So round a look he cast,
And seeing that they gained far more
  By stratagem, than strength,
He found a seat, which he secured
  By stretching out full length.

And being wise as well as apt,
  He held his own so well,
That, if 'twere in a better cause,
  I should be proud to tell ;
But when the ticket-puncher came,
  He left his line of ease,
And in the corner, sat as prim
  And innocent's you please.

But one thing there his vision met,
　　Which won upon his heart—
A mother, weary, needing rest,
　　Fulfilled a mother's part—
Forgot her own sad weariness,
　　And gave her thought and care
Unto her little weary son;
　　Oh! love, how sweet, how rare!

A mother's love! Oh, priceless gem!
　　Oh! mine of wealth untold!
I hold thee dearer than my life,
　　An hundred thousand fold.
All other love may fail, and prove
　　As naught but empty air;
But thou art true while life shall last,
　　Oh! love without compare.

The wee, uncertain, toddling steps,
　　Of tender infancy,
Are fondly watched, and watched full well,
　　When they are watched by thee;
And still in childhood's happy hours,
　　Sweet hours of joyous play,
How oft, to heav'n a prayer goes up,
　　To guard them on their way!

And still in youth and manhood's prime,
   When feelings stronger grow,
Thou watchest on, with tender glance,
   Where'er those feet may go ;
And still you cherish them as dear,
   Yes, dearer, day by day ;
And still thy prayer ascends on high,
   That they go not astray.

You scarcely feel that they have grown,
   They're still the same to you ;
The same you watched, in years agone,
   So faithful, fond and true,
And though they wander e'er so far,
   Thy wealth of tenderness,
Thro' years of time shall never change,
   Nor e'er shall it grow less.

But, goodness gracious ! bless my eyes !
   To you it must be plain,
Instead of writing mirth, I've struck
   A sentimental vein.
But to the one who reading this,
   Would praise to me award,
As Byron says : "Ah ! reader mine,
   I spin this by the yard."

But John had eyes for other things
  Than this fond mother's love ;
A smiling face and tender eye
  Did now his soft heart move ;
The train had at a station stopped,
  A maiden entered in,
And all alone she seemed to be,
  Which John condemned a sin.

She took the seat before the one
  In which our Hero sat,
The only one which vacant was,
  And John was glad of that ;
For thus he had a splendid chance,
  Her beauty to admire ;
To open conversation then
  Be sure, was his desire.

But he had been too well brought up,
  For anything like that,
And so contented him to sit
  Admiring while he sat ;
But, by and by, the maiden turned,
  And sweetly wished to know,
If he would kindly tell how far
  It was —— to some depot.

Now John was taken so aback,
  By her sweet words and smiles,
He answered what he wished was true,
  " About a thousand miles ;"
Now as they were not half that way,
  From New York City vast,
No wonder that the maid on him,
  A look of doubting cast.

John saw his error, and in haste
  Excuses stammered out,
And said he wondered what he could
  Be thinking then about ;
Then told the distance, as it was,
  Well pleased o'er what he'd done,
For conversation, by this slight
  Mistake, was well begun.

They talked about the weather, and
  The pleasures of the way ;
And suchlike other senseless things,
  Which some folks find to say ;
Now John, whose heart was very soft,
  Was easily impressed ;
And little knew that maiden, of
  The tumult in his breast.

But one had marked it well indeed,
   An ancient, straight-backed maid ;
She saw how things were going on,
   And plans to stop them laid;
She rose, like " bird of prey" and down
   Beside the maiden lights ;
Then says to John : " Young man, do you
   Believe in Woman's Rights ?"

Now had a bolt of thunder burst
   At John's astonished feet,
It had not more dismayed him, than
   That bolt within the seat ;
The thunder of his maddened no,
   The very seats did jar ;
And with a look of hatred deep,
   He rose and left the car.

But back to travel let us go,
   The breakfast comes apace ;
Just twenty minutes now you have,
   To eat and wash your face ;
And just as you've begun to eat,
   " Time's up," is loudly roar'd ;
You scald your throat with red-hot tea,
   In haste to get aboard.

The dinner, too, is just the same,
   You're forced to run away
With just one fiith the worth of what
   You may have had to pay ;
But every journey has an end,
   And this was like the rest ;
From " Little Rhody," to New York,
   Is but a day at best.

And so, at last, mid rush and roar,
   He entered on the pave,
And wondered much, to see the folks
   So solemn look and grave ;
For every one just looked as though
   They would increase the pace,
Or just as if their very life
   Depended on the race.

But with the crowd he sped along,
   Till Broadway met his view ;
But this a little too much proved,
   For scarce could he get through ;
The rush, the roar, the oath, the jest,
   The rolling, rumbling sound,
Composed a Babel so immense,
   One's mind it might confound.

As through the crowd he shoved his way,
   With wonder he did gaze
Upon the stores, mile after mile,
   And on their grand displays;
And when he saw the countless throng
   In each direction dash,
He wondered where they all got knives,
   To eat their little hash.

'Mid big hotels, and grand saloons.
   The pride of great Broadway,
He wandered on, and wondered much
   Where he was going to stay ;
At last he saw a little "Inn,"
   Which made him lightly laugh ;
But found the price per day, alas !
   Three dollars and a half.

" Lord bless my eyes !" says John, "but you
   Have got a mighty cheek."
" Why sir, at home, for that sum, I
   Could almost board a week."
He left, and strolling down the street,
   Came to the Brandreth House,
Whose wondrous size, and well kept look,
   His fancy did arouse.

"I wonder now," our Hero said,
    "What they would charge per day ;
Three dollars and a half, that scrub
    Would have a fellow pay ;
If board in such a place as yon,
    Is worth that sum, why then
The tariff at this stylish place,
    Should sure be all of Ten."

Says he then to himself, "I think
    I'll go and ask for fun."
So in he went, for 'twas with him
    No sooner said than done,
But "muchly" he was taken back,
    And great was his surprise,
Confounded at the bear "idee,"
    And thunderstruck likewise.

The clerk, a gentlemanly chap,
    Our Hero's question heard,
"'Tis by the day a dollar, sir,"
    This was his very word.
John thought he had not heard aright
    So asked the clerk again,
And found to his unfeigned delight,
    The fact was true and plain.

" By jingo !" said our Hero then,
 " I think I'd better stay,
For board so cheap, I have not seen
 I cannot tell the day.
Good gracious ! if the Cataract,
 And Fulton's Hotel too,
Would only follow up this plan,
 What business they might do !"

Well, supper time came on apace,
 And John quite hungry grew,
So thought he'd seek the Dining-room,
 And put the victuals through ;
He found the place, began to eat,
 Got just whate'er he wished,
He did the supper justice, just,
 And many dishes, dished.

So when he thought he'd ate enough,
 And felt quite well indeed,
He thought he'd take a tramp around,
 To settle down his feed,
But when he reached the door was stopped
 Politely, by a man,
To find the House was kept upon,
 The "European Plan."

Some may not know what this may be,
  And such I will enlight ;
'Tis pay for what you eat and drink,
  Your dollar's for the night ;
Well John of course could not demur,
  So paid his little bill ;
Then out, to "do" the city went,
  As greenhorns always will.

Down Broadway to the City Hall,—
  This was the course he took ;
Then down among the printing Sts.,
  He thought he' take a look ;
Here, where the Papers issued are,
  Editions every hour,
Is where the News-boys congregate,
  And's called the devil's bower.

But growing late, he thought a trip
  To Wallack's he would take ;
Where he had heard, a Comic Play
  Did mirthfulness awake ;
He saw the artist, Emmet, there,
  Who made some pointed hits,
Upon the immigration in
  Our German Cousin " Fritz."

He saw how poor way-farers, from
  The " Land beyond the sea,"
Were dealt with, when they reached this land
  Of wealth and liberty;
But Fritz a hero proved himself—
  Ere many years had passed,
Turned " miller," and a fortune made,
  And came out right at last.

But Plays, like other things, must end,
  So this was quickly o'er—
Then out on Broadway with a rush,
  The folks began to pour ;
But while the Play was going on,
  A storm had risen high,
And now, in grand sublimity,
  The thunderbolts did fly.

Sublime, no doubt, but just to John,
  Who had his best clothes on,
He, doubtless, better had been pleased,
  Had it been passed and gone ;
The thunder roared, the lightning flashed,
  The torrents poured—" you bet!"
And John, poor devil, in a wink,
  Got most sublimely wet.

And as he didn't drink, you know,
  Some solace there he lacked,
The bad effects of getting wet,
  He couldn't counteract;
For by some queer contrariness,
  'Tmay seem to you and I,
Some dry themselves with drink when wet,
  And drink when they are dry.

But now our Hero went to bed,
  Quite tired and sleepy too,
Dreampt wondrous dreams, of what upon
  The morrow he would do—
Next morning he was up,—though not
  Exactly with the lark—
And after breakfast, took a stroll
  To see the "Central Park."

Great Central Park! ah! well indeed,
  May folks be proud of thee!
Thy pleasant rambles, and thy walks,
  Are fraught with witchery.
No European city, grand,
  Can match thy beauties rare;
Thy lovely bowers, and sylvan shades,
  We ne'er can meet with there.

New York may boast of countless wealth,
   Of millionaires in scores,
And point with pride unto her wharves,
   Her shipping and her shores—
But all as nothing do they count,
   Unto the Poet's mind—
'Tis all but dross, till in thy shade,
   True riches he doth find.

Thus in a world-forgetting strain,
   Our Hero mused, as he
Meandered mid the sylvan wealth,
   And sylvan witchery;
Here, where no sound of busy life
   Disturbs the resting ear,
Enchantment seems to reign supreme,
   No harsh discordance near.

The "Arbor!"—well 'tis rightly named,
   Its clinging vines around
So softly stirred, by gentlest breezes,
   And trailing on the ground,
Bear to our minds an emblem, of
   What woman's love may be,
And is, if we by Poet's judge,
   "True clinging frailitie."

Clinging, 'tis said—well, yes, just there,
　　Poets and I agree;
They cling enough, that, goodness knows;
　　In fact too much for me.
I've heard it said, that woman's love
　　Of tenderness is born ;
"And like the ivy to the oak,
　　Clings closest in the storm."

Well that may be, I'll not dispute,
　　Though I am not so tuned ;
I think, in fact, the more they cling,
　　Why just the more we're ruined ;
Now if some sweet, bewitching maid
　　Should chance to read this note,
Mayhap she'd like with force to twist
　　A rope around my throat.

But bless you ! ladies, save your wrath—
　　I didn't mean a word.
In writing, I'm like some folks, who
　　Keep talking to be heard ;
And though you may our fortunes break,
　　And cause us heartaches sore,
And spend the cash with spareless hand,
　　We'll love you all the more.

For who, in wild delirium's hour,
  Can smooth the fevered brow
With hand so soft, and gentle touch.
  Ah! woman, none but thou!
But here I go, confound the luck,
  At sentiment again!
I'm like a car that's off the track,
  For I am off the strain.

So back again, I'll go as fast
  As ever I can go ;
And some queer things, the which befell
  Our Hero, try to show.
He slept quite sound last night, I ween
  That fact you need not doubt,
For with his love and anger, he
  Was just about played out.

So he arose refreshed, indeed,
  And feeling better quite ;
But still the mem'ry of that maid
  Held to his fancy tight.
Ah! memory, thou art truer far,
  Than ever one would deem—
Things lost to view within thy cells,
  Still fresh and green doth seem!

A single smile, a simple word,
  By friend all thoughtless given,
Thou holdest long, nor can it from
  Thy truthful trust be driven ;
A harsh rebuke, perchance, may seem
  To pass unheeded by ;
But long, within thy inmost depths,
  'Twill like a canker lie.

Then take ye heed, ye thoughtless ones,
  And give no harsh word forth ;
A gentle word will nothing cost,
  And sure will prove more worth ;
Remember, that whate'er you give,
  For cause of joy or pain,
In just such measure as ye mete,
  'Twill meted be again

But now, our Hero on his tramp,
  We'll follow at our ease ;
We may find something to instruct,
  Or something that may please.
The Central Park he strolled around,
  Admired its beauties rare,
Its little cascades, lakes and rills,
  Of which it hath its share.

Now here, one small digression more,
    I pray that you'll permit—
The scene reminds me of an one,
    Which I shall ne'er forget.
'Tis where Niagara in its might,
    Its cliffs of grandeur show ;
Where swift its waters rushing on,
    Forever, ceaseless, flow.

Here, in my youth—at sixteen, say,
    I deeply fell in love
With one, who in my heart I thought
    An angel from above.
I loved her, with a love which I
    Considered true and pure ;
Which like the mountains of the earth,
    Forever might endure.

Though she a little older was,
    Than I, a beardless youth,
I offered her my heart and hand,
    And did it, too, in truth ;
She didn't laugh, but softly said
    In words which my heart wrung,
"No doubt you mean just what you say,
    But Johnnie, you're too young."

This damped my ardor, but for all
   I didn't quite despair ;
For women of sweet coaxing like,
   In fact a goodly share.
But when I very urgent grew,
   And sore my suit did press,
She gave me as an answer, what
   Made greater my distress.

She said my answer I should find
   In Samuel 2nd part,
Tenth Chapter, and in verse the fifth.
   I found what broke my heart,
Which was, "Until your beard be grown
   Tarry at Jericho."
Now, don't you wonder how I e'er
   Withstood that dreadful blow?

Well, but I did, and oft' again
   Engaged in Cupid's war ;
Sometimes successful, and sometimes
   Received on heart a scar,
But as I don't intend this book,
   Shall of *my* doings treat ,
We'll move along and follow John,
   As he goes down the street.

Down Broadway, then down Liberty
  To Greenwich thoroughfare,
To view a rail road set on stilts
  For travel in the air;
He found that on account of some
  Sad accidents of late,
The railway, for the present, was
  Abandoned to its fate.

So, as he couldn't travel up,
  He thought he'd travel down,
And fell into a lottery pit,
  Like any country clown,
He had a sort of greenish look,
  Which "Cappy" soon discerned,
Who straightway laid a trap to win
  The money John had earned.

In came a tall, slim-looking chap,
  Who, wonder-struck, did gaze
Upon the shelves and counter, which
  With gold were all ablaze ;
The clerk, polite as one could wish,
  Low bowed, and smiling said,
"Now is the time to try your luck,
  Take hold and go ahead."

"Here gold and silver watches are,
  I might say thrown away ;
Rich jewelry, of the finest kind
  And nothing but fair play."
The slim man laid a dollar down,
  And gave the dice a fling,
And drew—could he believe his eyes ?
  A cluster diamond ring.

He tried again, his luck was good,
  A silver watch he drew ;
He still kept throwing, and his luck
  Each time still better grew ;
Gold coins and watches, rings and chains,
  He took at every hitch,—
John said, "at this rate, you, my friend,
  Will soon be getting rich."

He smiled; and said, "Well, so it seems,
  But then, I'm not a hog,
Just take a chance, and see if you
  Are such a lucky dog."
John said, "Oh, no ! I would not break
  Your luck in such a way ;
You're doing well, pray, go ahead,
  The business seems to pay."

But no, the tall, slim-looking man
    Thought he had won enough,
And said he didn't want to use
    The firm so deuced rough.
To importune our Hero then,
    The clerk did soon begin ;
"But no," said John, "your game, my friend
    'S a little bit too thin."

The clerk and capper both chagrined,
    Had not a word to say,
Except those two emphatic ones,
    Which simply were, "*good day.*"
But which, to one who in his life
    Had traveled some about,
Might be interpreted to mean,
    "You dirty dog, git out."

John, knowing that discretion was
    Firm valor's better part,
Got up the dirty steps in style,
    That might be counted smart ;
He turred up " Liberty" again,
    And here a place passed by,
Where sat a little sickly girl
    With wistful pleading eye.

Her story ran a little thus :
　When our cruel war was o'er,
And treason had its death blow felt,
　From shore to distant shore,
Some rascals, to all pity dead,
　Had ruthlessly deprived
Her mother of the means, from which
　Her living she derived.

And now, her health had left her too,
　And she at death's door lay,
Dependant on her little girl,
　For bread from day to day.
The story touched our Hero's heart,
　So sad was her appeal ;
He gave a dollar, and for this
　Small act did better feel.

Perchance the story was all false,
　Yet, may be, it was true ;
Far better lose a dollar, than
　Do that, the which we'd rue.
A little gift in time of need,
　A recompense may gain
Of prayers, which we may not feel
　Yet may not be in vain.

Oh, speak not harsh unto the poor,
    Who daily beg their bread ;
For life is sad enough to those,
    Who cold and hunger dread.
A kindly word is never lost,
    Though it unheeded fall ;
Tho' words and smiles may nothing cost,
    They may an answer call.

Oh, give ye then, unto the poor
    A kindly word and smile ;
Sad, gloomy thoughts they may dispel,
    And cheer a heart the while ;
A burdened soul may sigh and sink
    Beneath a load of grief;
And wealth might fail, where kindly words
    Would bring a calm relief.

Oh ! little know ye of the power.
    Ye daily cast aside,
Who harshly scorn the supplicant,
    And all his woes deride ;
Oh ! if ye have not wealth to give,
    Give what you have the while ;
'Tis something that you cannot miss,
    A kindly word and smile.

But as the folks in business say,
  "Quick sales and profits small ;"
To keep this Canto longer on
  The stocks, wont do at all.
And wishing John a good night's rest,
  We'll bid to him adieu :
In hopes to meet again, upon
  The "Vanderbilt" or "Drew."

END OF CANTO I.

CANTO II.

There's nought but care on ev'ry han;
  In ev'ry hour that passes, O; |
What signifies the life o' man
  An' twa na for the lasses, O?

The warly race may riches chase
  An' riches still may fly them, O;
An' tho' at last they catch them fast,
  Their hearts can ne'er enjoy them, O.

But gie me a cannie hour at e'en
  My arms about my dearie, O;
An' warly cares an' warly men
  May a' gae tapsalteerie, O.
                              —BURNS.

Another day—the afternoon
  Is wearing to a close;
John knows full well the boat for him
  To wait does not propose.
He grabbed his luggage, and in haste,
  For Spring Street made a dash;
Played porter for himself, and there—
  By saved a little cash.

He reached the dock, and just in time,
  The deck hands there he found
Were throwing luggage in a style
  Which might be counted sound,
But which would show to those who care
  To keep their baggage long
That trunks, valises and such things
  Could ne'er be made too strong.

But seeing nothing there in which
  He any interest had,
It did n't hurt his feelings much
  To see them used so bad.
He found the boat on which he took
  His passage up, to be
The " Vanderbilt," and just as staunch
  As he's proclaimed to be.

Folks freely boast the wond'rous power
  Of this great Railway King,
And far from Democratic-like
  His quandam praises sing.
A palace car is being built ;
  The builder, all aflame,
With tho'ts of this great " thunderbolt,"
  Must make it bear his name.

A new hotel is going up,
　　And scarce ere it be done,
The painter comes with paint and brush,
　　As if for life he'd come.
In haste he plasters o'er the front,
　　Big letters, plain or gilt,
To let folks know that this might be
　　The house that Vander-*bilt*.

A horse that never ran before,
　　A country race may win ;
His owner, in elation great,
　　Thinks it would be a sin
His pacer should not have a name,
　　When other horses can ;
And so the world is better, for
　　Another lightning " Van."

Perhaps the mania soon will grow
　　To such a great extent,
That anything without a " Van"
　　Will not be worth a cent.
And by-and-by, how oft, as we
　　Along the street may go,
That name may meet our eye and ear,
　　The Lord alone may know.

But Railway Kings, like other kings,
  Their power often lose ;
And those who praise him loudest now,
  May just as loud abuse
For some go up, while some come down,
  Dame Fortune is an elf,
But as the veteran Tweed has said,
  " You know how 'tis yourself."

But there, I think I've said enough !
  Perhaps more than I should ;
I scarce can hope my simple rhyme
  Will do a mite of good.
So here the subject I will leave,
  And with my pen return
Unto our Hero, and recite
  What new things he may learn.

Well, 'mid the rush on board the boat
  For state rooms and the like ;
He saw a lady striving hard
  To breast the human dyke
And gain the office window, where
  Her passage she might pay ,
But still those " horrid masculines,"
  Would push her far away.

But John, just like a gallant chap,
  Gave helping hand in style;
For which, he from the lady won
  A sweet and thankful smile.
And as the lady was quite fair,
  And seemed to be alone,
He into conversation fell
  With rather friendly tone.

I said the lady was quite fair,
  Now she was small as well;
So, cannot blame our Hero, if
  In love he quickly fell.
I like small women,—but just why
  I'm sure I cannot say,
Perhaps there is no reason—but
  I like them any way.

The Lady and our Hero then
  Upon the upper deck,
Watched New York, till as some folks say,
  It grew into a speck.
They chatted gaily of the scenes
  Which all around them lay;
John gave his name—she did the same,
  Her name was Jennie Grey.

Sing-Sing! melodeous name indeed!
　　Alas! how sad a thing,
To think upon the many there
　　Who never care to sing!
Shut out, in fact, from all the world,
　　Or ratherwise shut in,
Because, perchance they killed some one—
　　As though that were a sin.

If they had lived in times like these,
　　With things at such advance,
With lawyers of the present day,
　　They might have stood a chance ;
And " momentarily insane,"
　　The verdict might have been,
(Of course, what crazy people do,
　　Cannot be called a sin.)

The conversation still between
　　Our Hero and Miss Grey,
Was kept up as the boat went on,
　　In rather lively way.
It seems Miss Grey had traveled some,
　　And read a great deal too,
And had a fascinating way
　　Of telling what she knew.

John did his best to hold his own,
    And spoke and smiled by turns,—
Grew rapt'rous and to quoting took,
    From Byron, Moore and Burns;
He even went so far as to
    Recite some of his own,
And much surprised himself, to see
    How eloquent he'd grown.

By this time they had reached West Point;
    The cradle where were rocked
Some of the great war intellects,
    Which proud Rebellion shocked.
Here, in the Nation's school of war,
    Our youthful heroes learn
That science dread, which yet for them,
    Undying fame may earn.

Yet is it fair, I ask, that they,
    Whose fathers nobly fought
For that which to the Contraband
    His long sought freedom brought,
Should banish from their ranks, in scorn,
    One who may loyal be,
Because his blood, from Afric's tint,
    May not be wholly free?

I hold that such things should not be,
  Though no dispute I'd wake ;
Yet less than this has often put
  A Nation's weal at stake,
And trifling though the matter seem
  'Tis fraught with weal or woe ,
A Nation's footing may be lost,
  Through stepping on a toe.

But let that go, sometime, perchance,
  In Democratic range,
The order of these little things
  May undergo a change.
But thoughts like these could scarce engross
  Our youthful Hero's mind,
For he in mystic love's sweet charms,
  Had left such thoughts behind.

Oh ! ye who never felt the power.
  Of that most potent charm,
Can scarcely know the weight it wields
  For mighty good or harm !
Oh ! would ye learn, ye skeptical,
  Love's mighty mystic power,
Just up the Hudson take a trip
  At twilight's witching hour !

While through the west the golden beams,
    Resplendent from the sun,
Send all their amber glory up
    To say the day is done,
Have by your side a youthful maid,
    Both fair of face and form,
I pledge you that the power of love
    Full soon your heart will warm.

But John, whose heart for love you know
    Was aye a tender seat,
'Neath glances sweet from Jennie Gray,
    Flew up to fever heat.
In fact, I really think he lost
    The little sense he had,
And, it the trip a thousand miles
    Had been, he'd sure been glad.

The hours unheeded passed along,
    All free from gloom or care,
For what could mar a scene like this?
    Alas! that joy's so rare!
Why cannot pleasure always last,
    Why cometh sorrow's tear?
Alas! why should misfortune fall
    On man from year to year?

"Man lives to mourn" alas! how true!
 His life a simple breath,
He comes and goes, he knows not how,
 ·'Tis simply life and death.
Oh! vain and futile all the strife
 For worldly wealth and fame;
'Tis folly sure, to strive for what
 At best is but a name.

Oh! could mankind the warning heed,
 Of millions gone before,
How better far the retrospect
 Would be when life is o'er!
But so it has been from the first,
 And doubtless so 'twill be,
Till chaos holds again the sway
 O'er lifeless land and sea.

"But whither would my fancy go"?—
 This moralizing strain
Is rather foreign to my way:
 I'll to my tale again,
·And tell how John, as they drew near
 To Albany, flew round
Until the countless packages,
 Which Jennie had, were found.

How Jennie grew profuse with thanks,
  As faster still he flew,
And wondered, if 'twere not for him,
  How ever she'd got through.
Her silv'ry words soft rippling o'er
  Her lips of cherry red,
Were pure enchantment, and enough
  To turn our Hero's head.

And as the Boat was tying up,
  And crowds began to press,
John threw his arm around her, And—
  Could any one do less?
He gathered all her parcels up,—
  A dozen, less or more,—
And, like a pack mule o'er the plank,
  Made way to gain the shore.

"Now here," says Jennie, "we must part,
  But you I'll ne'er forget,
And always bear in mem'ry fond
  The pleasant day we met."
With beating heart John then did say,
  "Let me the pleasure take
Of seeing you in safety home,—
  E'en for that meeting's sake."

"Oh! no! to thus intrude upon
   Your time it is not meet ;
Besides, there is my husband, now,
   Just coming down the street."
"Your husband !"–"yes ; why not"?–"oh!—ah !
   That is !—ahem !—good day !
I can't conveniently assist ;
   I haven't time to stay."

Then round the corner, down the street,
   He quick did disappear ;
While still in silvery cadence sweet,
   Her laugh rang in his ear,
Poor John ! alas ! alas ! poor John !
   His luck seems out of joint ;
For every pleasure that he meets
   Is sure to disappoint.

He gained the depot just in time
   To take the Western train ;
While in his heart he swore no more
   In love to fall again.
But foolish youth ! he little knew
   How wayward is the heart,
Which, "homeopathic-like," doth try
   To cure a smart with smart.

And so, ere he had been an hour
    Upon his westward way,
A pair of eyes of midnight hue,
    Their batteries had at play.
Yet not the eyes alone made war,
    For features aided them,
O'er which a sculptor might go mad,
    A Poet wildly dream.

But hark! what cry is that so wild
    That it unearthly seems?
The brakemen rush unto their posts,
    The engine shrieks and screams,
Folks run to window and to door,
    Confused and in alarm,
Filled with a wild dread undefined
    Of some impending harm.

A moment's halt, then on its way
    The train again is bound,
But still there lingers in the ear
    That wild unearthly sound.
And words of pity, spoken low,
    On every side are heard;
But John sees only one fair form,
    And hears alone her word.

She takes her seat with haughty mien,
  'Mid looks enquiring cast,
And answers, cold and unconcerned
  While questions round are passed,
"Only a dirty laborer
  Has had his leg cut off."
God!—how scornful was the tone!
  How well attuned to scoff!

Only a dirty laborer!
  What matter for his life,
His children crying mournfully,
  His sorrow stricken wife?
She is a queen of fashion,
  On fashion's sea afloat;
He is a dirty laborer,
  Unworthy of her note.

Only a dirty laborer!
  A plebeian, poor, untaught!
Only a dirty laborer!
  Unworthy of a thought.
From henceforth all unable
  To win his daily bread—
Not even a dirty loborer—
  Better that he were dead.

Yet *was* he a dirty laborer,
　　To that sorrow-stricken wife?
He whose tender words and smiles,
　　Had lessened cares of life?
A kind and loving husband,
　　Bringing sunshine to his door,
Was he a dirty laborer?
　　Just that, and nothing more.?

Was he a dirty laborer,
　　To the children crying low,
Loving and kind and tender,
　　Watching them upward grow?
Ever a loving father,
　　Leading them up life's way,
Was he a dirty laborer,
　　Think you, to them to day?

Was he a dirty laborer,
　　To God who rules above,
Whose every thought is goodness,
　　Whose every word is Love?
When he gathers his precious jewels
　　Now scattered far and wide,
Because he's a dirty laborer,
　　Will one be cast aside?

Well, I am not judge of actions,
  I have no word to say ;
But John, whom I'd most forgotten,
  And I, felt alike that day ;
And, being so mad that he then
  From swearing scarce could keep,
He kicked up the cushion endways,
  Laid down and went to sleep.

How long he slept he knew not,
  But near the close of day,
The Conductor woke him up and
  Took his ticket away.
And he knew that he was nearing
  The place he came to view ;
And he shook himself like Samson
  For strength to see him through.

But hark ! what is that rumbling sound,
  That dreadful deaf'ning roar !
Is that the noise the waters make
  As o'er the Falls they pour !
The train has stopped, John rushes forth
  Amid the deaf'ning shout,
To find that it is nothing but
  The porters calling out,

"This way for the International!"
  "Pass in your checks to me!"
"Go to the Cataract, if you'd like
  The Falls with ease to see!"
"Pass right through to the Spencer House!"
  "Niagara House this way!"
Each yelling, as if each would drown
  What each one had to say.

But John concluded not to ride,
  So through the depot ran;
And here, alas! poor foolish youth,
  His troubles just began.
For ere he steps upon the walk
  A score of hackmen call,
"Jump in! 'twill only cost five cents
  To ride down to the Fall."

'Twas easy seen that John was green,
  They pounced upon their prey,
They gathered round him by the score,
  Thus blocking up the way.
And like a pack of wolves that snap
  And haggle o'er a bone,
Each strove to carry off the "seed,"
  Each claimed him as his own.

They called each other robbers, thieves,
    And rogues and liars, too ;
It was a shame to hear such names,
    I hope they were not true.
They swore so much, and swore so loud,
    As each his tongue–lash plied,
The very air grew sulph'rous, and
    Poor John grew terrified.

He saw an opening in the crowd,
    The way before was plain ;
So thro' the gap and down the street,
    He dashed with might and main.
His hat fell off, his coat tail spread,
    I vow 'twas like a fan,
And "Gilpin's Ride" was *nothing* to
    The way our Hero ran.

An urchin on the street cried out,
    " Mad dog !" and " clear the way !"
A hundred tongues took up the cry;
    The devil was to pay.
But John, unheeding, passed along
    And reached the Ferry Grove,
And there beneath a tree sank down,
    With scarcely strength to move.

And there he lay till eventide ;
    Then through the busy town,
He sought a place of lodging
    And gulped his supper down.
Then dragged his weary form to bed,
    More tired than he'd been yet,
While nightmare hackmen by the score,
    His peaceful rest upset.

END OF CANTO II.

CANTO III.

Clown—Have I not told thee how I was
    cozened by the way, and lost
    all my money ?

Autolycus—And, indeed, sir, there are
    cozeners abroad, therefore
    it behooves one to be wary.

                     —SHAKESPEARE.

Winter's Tale, Act IV , Scene III.

Up in the morning early
  Ere day was well begun,
John started forth to see the sights
  E'en with the rising sun.
But early though he took the road
  A "hack" was there as well ;
And long the driver followed him
  And great things he did tell.

He said to John that he would show
　　To him a view ful! rare
For five cents, and the trip should be
　　Made in that carriage there.
John thought that that was cheap enough
　　And therefore did agree;
He jumped into the hack and down
　　That rare sight went to see.

John said I don't see how, my friend,
　　You make this business pay,
To live at all you surely must
　　Make many trips a day;
Or else for making money you
　　Must have some other ways.
The driver smiled a queerish smile
　　And simply said, it pays.

By this time they had reached a place
　　Where rainbows could be seen
Which in the early morning were
　　Full beautiful I ween;
John gazed with admiration deep
　　Upon the rapids grand,
Which up in seeming merriment
　　Leapt high on every hand.

The driver broke John's rapture up
   By asking him if he
Would like to see the Falls in all
   Their mighty majesty.
He said no good view could be had
   Unless they went *around*;
But *there* grand beauty unexcelled
   Could easily be found.

John said " all right, we'll drive around,
   I came the Falls to view,
And hang me if I don't intend
   To see the whole thing through."
Poor foolish youth, his verdancy
   Would make a cynic laugh,
Most anyone would be content
   With seeing less than half.

But round they went and o'er the Bridge
   And into Canada;
I'll guarantee John ne'er forgets
   The trip he made that day.
And here allow me to remark
   This game is often played,
They call it " turning," and God help
   You when that " turn " is made.

They cross the Bridge then down the bank
  The Table Rock to view,
And here is where the " Native Sharks "
  Commence to "put you through."
Ere John had from the carriage stepped
  A chap came out to know
If he would like a picture of
  Himself and Falls also.

John asked the price, but not a word
  Could he get in reply,
But round about with plates prepared
  The operators fly;
And in a twinkling they turn out
  A sight would make you laugh,
For which they tax poor simple John
  Four dollars and a half.

Into the Table Rock House next
  Poor John is soon betrayed,
And there they put him through as if
  The devil lent his aid;
They show him Indian relics which
  The Indians never saw;
John buys a lot of things for which
  He does not care a straw.

John begs the driver to depart
 Ere he be ruined quite,
But ere a dozen rods are made
 He's doomed to re-alight.
And now the " Museum " minions
 Around him quickly swarm,
And ere he's well upon his feet
 He's dragged in by the arm.

They wrap him up in oilcloth robes
 Ere he be well aware,
And o'er the street they hurry him
 To take him down the stair ;
John grabbed the railing and in words
 By desperation lent,
Demanded of his captors grim
 What they in thunder meant ?

They told him they were taking him
 Behind the waterfall,
And that the way was easy and
 Not dangerous at all.
Still hanging on he asked how much
 For *this* he'd have to pay ;
" Just give the guide whate'er you wish,
 That is the gen'ral way."

So John let go and followed them
    Along the winding way,
But little worth for money spent
    Did he get there that day.
His feet got wet, his boots got spoilt,
    Likewise his collar too,
He gave the guides each fifty cents
    To see that humbug view.

Then through the Museum he is led
    And all the wonders shown,
Gathered from every spot on earth
    From every land that's known.
They lead him through the office then
    As butchers lead a calf,
And when he starts to go they say
    Two dollars and a half.

" Two dollars and a half," says John,
    " Good gracious! what for now ?
I haven't bought a single thing
    I'm sure you will allow."
" Two dollars of the sum is for
    Your trip behind the sheet,
And fifty cents the Museum through
    Just makes the sum complete."

" Oh but," says John, "I paid the guides,
   I cannot pay you twice."
" That's nought to us," the "shark" replies,
   " 'Two dollars is our price."
" Tis robbery I swear," says John,
   " I'll pay it if I must,
Of all the 'beats' that ever beat,
   You beat the very worst."

Then to the Battle Ground he went,
  · The Burning Spring as well,
Another dollar from his purse,
   Which now had lost its swell.
The forenoon now was well nigh gone
   And John had hungry grown,
His watch proclaimed this certain fact
   Five hours had nearly flown.

Then homeward they in haste did drive,
   They landed safe and sound;
John searched his pockets through and soon
   A five cent piece he found;
Then to the driver he did hand
   That five cent nickel piece;
The driver took it—turned it o'er,
   And said " pray what is this?"

"Why that is for the ride" said John,
    "The bargain was, you know,
The Falls and all the views around
    For five cents you would show."
"Five cents be d—d," the driver said,
    "I guess I'll make you sneeze,
Perhaps you take me for a "flat;"
Ten dollars if you please."

"Oh Lord !" says John, "you heartless wretch!
    I ne'er was used so sore,
You saw me robbed along the way
    A dozen times or more,
But ne'er a warning you did give,
    No word for me you had,
And now you rob me worst of all,
    This really is too bad."

" I saw you robbed along the way ?"
    " Well, yes," the driver said,
" But why should I give warning when
    I got the half you paid.
I did n't care a cuss so long
    'S your pocket book held out,
If I had seen it running low
    You bet I'd turned about."

" But don't imagine that I take
    A cent more than is right,
The law allows me what I ask
    I don't o'ercharge a mite,
Here are (established by the law)
    Our latest rates of fare,
Just read them o'er and you will find
    My charge is fair and square."

John pulled his pocket-book out slow
    And laid the money down,
" From this time I will ride no more
    While I am in the town."
Then off to dinner he did go
    Which was made ready soon,
Then by himself he strolled away
    To spend the afternoon.

I said our Hero swore that he
    No more would ride again,
But ere he'd traveled many rods
    It proved his oath was vain ;
A driver stopped him on the way
    And offered to convey
Him round Goat Island for the which
    Two dollars he should pay.

The day was very warm and John
    Concluded he would ride,
So o'er the Bridge he soon was whirled
    And down the Island side,
At Luna Island first they stopped,
    A wondrous sight I ween,
For here whene'er the moon is full
    The "Lunar Bow" is seen.

And here our Hero met with some
    Of that fast fading race,
The remnant of an Indian tribe
    Who dwell near-by this place.
Alas! poor Tuscaroras! you
    Will soon be swept away,
E'en now the White Man till the graves
    Where erst your Chieftains lay.

I heard one of these Natives sing
    A song most mournfully,
Some other poet heard it and
    Translated it for me.
I wish that I could give his name
    It ought to live full long,
But as I cannot give you that
    I'll give you this,——

THE SONG !
Alas! said an Indian,
I once had a home,
And a fair forest field
Where the wild deer could roam,
Where the Sachems could feast
On a festival day;
But the steel of the White Man
Hath swept them away,
 Hath swept them away.

I once had a Father
The guide of my youth,
And a Mother who taught me
The precepts of truth,
But their spirits have vanished
And cold is their clay,
For the steel of the White Man
Hath swept them away,
 Hath swept them away.

I once had a Sister
The pride of the vale,
And a Brother whose features
Were rugged and hale,
Who oft-times would join me
In innocent play,
But the steel of the White Man
Hath swept them away,
 Hath swept them away.

I once loved a Maiden
But where is she now?
The cold damps of death
Have long since laid her low;
Her home, friends and kindred
Have fallen a prey,
And the steel of the White Man
Hath swept them away,
   Hath swept them away.

And I stand alone now
The last of my race,
On this earth I find I
Have no more a place,
Since all that I cherished
Have fallen a prey,
And the steel of the White Man
Hath swept them away,
   Hath swept them away.

And I soon must follow
The "Great Spirit" will call
Me away to yon Land
Where the brave never fall;
To yon far distant shore
To yon fair forest shade
Where the steel of the White Man
Can never invade,
   Can never invade.

Ah Noble Savage! true, too true!
    The ruthless steel is driven;
Still onward strides the giant power
    'Gainst which you've vainly striven;
And still they sweep you from their path,
    And still you lose your sway,
While westward still the blazing star
    Of Empire takes its way.

But there, I swear, and do declare,
    I'm at my tricks again,
I wonder why I can't run by
    That sentimental vein;
I'm bowling on at Dexter speed,
    A sentiment will glow,
I look, enquire, and in the mire
    Heels over head I go.

But do not doubt, nor at me scout,
    Nor think this vain pretence,
I'll run this Canto out without
    Another word of sense.
And so from Luna Island now—
    The course our Hero finds—
We'll take a ten rod step and see
    The great "Cave of the Winds."

Here John was quiet politely asked
   If he would like to view
The wonders of this wondrous Cave
   And make the journey through ,
It crossed his mind that here he had
   Another humbug found,
And thought a dollar and a half
   Too much for being drowned.

But just as he was making up
   His mind to let it slip,
A party came along that seemed
   Determined on the trip.
Four ladies and two gentlemen
   Appeared to him not fair ;
So quick made up his mind that he
   The trip with them would share.

In jolly rigs of jolly make
   They soon were dressed complete,
While moccasins of dainty shape
   Encased their dainty feet;
The Guide came forward—made his bow,
   Then downward led the way,
Where soon Niagara in her mirth
   Baptised them with her spray.

The Guide arranged them at the Cave
  A Lady to each Gent,
Then down into the mighty pit
  With wary feet they went;
Oh how the wind did rush and roar!
  And how the spray did dash!
It seemed as tho' the earth had split;
  An endless, deaf'ning crash.

Just as tho' ten million minions
  Of Hades on a drunk,
Were rolling down into the pit
  A mountain, chunk by chunk.
Or just as tho' the mighty whole
  Great Alpine avalanche,
Had left its native mountain tops,
  Down sliding into France.

The Guide still onward led the way,
  Each Gent the outside took,
While Boreas in his wanton glee
  Their regimentals shook.
The Lady whom John had in charge
  Was just a little sprite,
A merry Water Nymph, John said,
  That nothing could affright.

And now they pass from out the Cave
    The two great Falls between;
Such grandeur and sublimity
    Can nowhere else be seen;
On right and left, the mighty walls
    Of water falling down,
In front, the sombre granite cliff
    O'erhanging like a frown.

Behind, the river foaming white,
    In fury wildly dashed,
High leaping 'gainst the rocks which it
    For centuries has washed ;
While round them flies the crystal spray,
    And o'er that mystic gown
Hangs with ten millions jewels set,
    Niagara's Rain Bow Crown.

They stand in reverential awe
    Within that circle grand,
And gaze upon the Master Work
    Of a mighty Master Hand.
Then down the path in single file
    Unto the river side,
Where panoramic like, the view
    Spreads out full far and wide.

There, on a rock, the which the Guide
    By name Jarohntou calls,
They view (where only can be viewed)
    The glory of the Falls ;
And, as they gaze, they wonder how
    Dame Nature could have got
So much of beauty so sublime
    All centered in one spot ?

John asked the Guide if that the rock
    On which they then did lean
Had not an Indian name, and if
    He knew what it might mean ?
The Guide replied it had, and that
    The meaning is, they say,
Remember the Guide when on the bank
    Your bill you come to pay !

They said they would, and then the Guide
    Unto the water took,
And went exploring "Sub-marine,"
    In every hole and nook;
And brought up for the Ladies there
    Such things as ne'er were seen,
Pebbles White, and Purple Shells,
    And Mermaid's Tresses Green.

Now John had learned the swimming art
  In Narragansett Bay,
So he "turned turtle" with the best
  From off the rock that day.
The others brought their Ladies' shells
  And pebbles by the quart,
And he of course could not do else
  Than prove himself as smart.

And so he dove while wonderstruck
  The native fishes fled,
And once he for his Lady brought
  A "bump upon his head."
But she declared that would not do,
  The merry little elf!
And so he found her something else
  And took it home himself.

Then o'er the Bridges, up the Bank,
  They press through misty rain,
And all declare themselves well pleased
  And vow they'll go again;
And when once more in christian clothes
  They find themselves arrayed,
The Guide for all his watchful care
  That day gets well repaid.

And now, all ye who visit here,
  See all the other views,
But never pass the Cave House by
  Nor to go through refuse.
And if you should be pressed for time
  And but an hour should have,
Why lay all other sights aside,
  And go and see the Cave.

No imposition there you'll find,
  For all is fair and square,
With everything in order kept
  And not a "runner" there.
And if that visit you should make
  And you are satisfied,
Why, when you come to pay your bill,
  Pray don't forget the Guide.

John found his carriage waiting still,
  So quickly to the Tower
He hastened on, and at this place
  One well might spend an hour.
For trembling on the very verge,
  Upheld by nought 'twould seem,
The Tower stands, a monument
  To mighty work supreme.

But John had lingered at the Cave
   The afternoon well through;
And so he scarce had time to catch
   A glimpse of this great view.
So taking but a hasty look
   And getting scarce alighted,
He hurried on to gaze upon
   "The Sisters Three United."

That is the way 'tis put by one
   Who fain would be a Poet,
Vide the "Buffalo Express,"
   His merit it doth show it.
But here one really does become
   Enamored of the scene,
Three Islands from the Main One out,
   Three Cataracts between.

Here years ago a single man
   At early morn would stray,
To watch the rising of the sun
   And revel in the spray,
Which rose and wreathed itself around
   The little cascade's brow;
From which it seems to bear the name
   Of "Hermit's Cascade" now.

But thirty years have changed the scene
 So wild and picturesque;
And Nature now to Art gives way
 Withal by Art is blest,
For o'er each little cataract
 A beauteous arch is thrown,
And now the Sister Islands stand
 United, all as one.

But as the afternoon is spent
 Our Hero thinks that he
Unto the town will now return
 To see what he can see.
And now it dawns upon his mind,
 That he had best prepare
To hold the driver to his price,
 Nor from it budge a hair.

And so two dollars he doth count,
 And when they reach the "stand,"
He hastes to put the money in
 The driver's outstretched hand.
The driver takes it, folds it up,
 In systematic way,
And with a pleasant "Thank you, sir,"
 He quickly drives away.

To say that John was much surprised
  Would not be much to say,
For this astonished him far more
  Than aught he'd seen that day;
And plainly showed, tho' he at first
  'Mong rascal drivers fell,
There are—tho' there be villains here—
  Some honest men as well.

The supper o'er John thro' the town
  Began to wander round,
And visit all the Indian Stores
  Where "notions" may be found.
He went thro' twenty stores at least,
  Saw fifty maidens fair,
But woe betide that visiting
  His money went like air.

For in each store he visited
  Some new thing he would spy,
The which, those "elfin, fairy clerks"
  Were sure to make him buy.
They'd hover round him till at last
  He'd lose his senses quite,
His tender heart could not say no,
  And thus they had him tight.

He bought—in every store he bought,
　His pockets he did fill,
His hat, his handkerchief, his hands,
　He filled and filled until,
If it had been on Christmas Eve
　Each passer by would pause,
And think for certain they had met
　Their childhood's Santa Claus.

But longest night must have an end,
　No lane but sometime turns,
And stores though multitudinous
　The last one he discerns.
Then one more item to the pile,
　A climax to the dome,
And groaning 'neath his mighty load
　At length he staggers home.

And when he got into his room
　His cargo he unshipped,
And overhauled his pocketbook
　To see how deep he'd dipped.
That pocketbook when he left home
　He filled from out the Bank;
But now, alas! 'twas changed indeed,
　And looked full lean and lank.

And thus its fate he did bewail,
    "Ah noble pocketbook !
Within thy spacious folds of yore
    My Father oft did look.
And oft have you been well puffed out,
    And oft have you been full,
And oft the strap which binds you up
    I've seen my Father pull."

"But never since my infancy
    Have you been half so thin,
Thy sides have lost their fullness and
    Thy face has lost its grin.
Thou lookest now as tho' some beast
    With elephantine tread;
Had set his monstrous foot upon
    Thy poor defenceless head."

" But, if I e'er get out of this,
    If ever I get home,
I'll be content with filling thee
    And seek no more to roam.
I've seen enough of travel now,
    I'll henceforth be content
To leave the wonders of the world
    To those on travel bent.

And now as to his virtuous couch
  Our Hero doth retire,
We'll say good night, put out the light,
  Hang up our unstrung lyre.
Our Hero needs a good night's rest,
  No one could wish him less,
This Canto's done, and I am glad,
  And, so are you, I guess.

END OF CANTO III.

CANTO IV.

Ho went like one that hath been stunn'd.
And is of sense forlorn:
A sadder and a wiser man
He rose the morrow morn.
—COLERIDGE.

The Lunar Bow! ah, beautiful!
   Just there, why I'll give in,
But 'mong the sights which I have seen
   With some it don't begin.
And how, to me 'tis scarcely plain,
   It came to have such fame,
To tell the truth, I really think
   There's something in a name.

The monlight though is not so bad,
   'Tis fan to watch the "swells,"
And then the fun's so much enhanced,
   By reason of the "belles,"
For every maid whom you here see,
   Though plain as any gnome,
Asserts in confidential way
   That she's the belle at home.

♦

Around the Isle at eventide,
  Oh, jolly ! ain't it fun ?
The scorching rays of Sol are gone,
  The rush and bustle done.
Here congregate the whole of all
  The pleasure seeking throng,
And echoes loud along the shore
  The gleeful laugh and song.

Now, this is where our Hero with
  His own thoughts did commune,
And strive to calm his troubled mind
  By converse with the moon.
Oh ! may be I forgot to tell
  His trouble, and its cause,
But, better late than never, still
  Is one of reason's laws.

Then first and foremost I'll begin,
  'Twas in the afternoon,
While strolling 'long the shore in quest
  Of sport, he found it soon.
A damsel fair—yes, truly fair
  As one would wish to see,
Unwitting any one was near,
  Went tripping merrily.

She wore a—well, I don't know what,
　I s'pose it was a hat,
But what the name, or style, or kind,
　No knowledge I've of that;
But suffice it for me to say,
　The dainty thing she wore,
Upon that memorable day
　Around Goat Island shore.

But 'Boreas' ever fitful, wild,
　Hatched in his noddle there
A scheme, by which he whipped away
　This hat into the air.
'Twas gone full twenty feet from shore,
　Repining was in vain,
No flood of tears, no lengthened pray'r,
　Could bring it back again.

She watched it with a woeful face
　As, dancing on a swell,
With undulations, up and down
　It gently rose and fell;
One moment near within her reach,
　Another, far away,
It seemed with glee of actual life
　To tantalizing play.

But John with faithful gallantry
  Soon to the rescue came,
And though with some discomfort, won
  The right her praise to claim.
He made a quick advance, and grasped
  The hat with movement neat,
He gained the hat,—and something else,
  And that was two wet feet.

He gave a sort of inward groan,
  And "blessed" his sad mischance,
Then at the author of it all
  He gave a sidelong glance;
Oh! she was pretty as a peach,
  And just as blooming too;
John lost his senses thro' that glance,
  And lost his heart anew.

She smiled a sweet, bewitching smile,
  Expressed her sorrow sore,
That she had been the cause of this
  Disaster on the shore;
That smile!—ah! what a power there is
  In one sweet, simple smile,
'Tis greater far than power of wealth,
  Or avaricious wile.

She spoke, and thralled him with her voice,
  Her thanks he scarce did hear,
The music seemed so ravishing
  Unto his love turned ear.
He managed just to stammer forth
  Some senseless commonplace,
He knew not what it was, nor cared,
  His soul was in his face.

Well, being all alone, you see,
  They could n't help but talk,
And John of course did nothing care
  How long she made the walk;
They wandered round the entire Isle,
  The sun was wearing low,
She murmured something about Aunt,
  Said she must homeward go.

John begged her leave to see her home,
  She couldn't well refuse,
Of course she could if that she would,
  Perhaps she did n't choose.
At any rate she gave consent,
  And John in glory was,
But wished that he had Joshua's power,
  To bid the sun to pause.

But knowing well that could not be,
　　Though deeming it too bad,
Ho thought he'd better make the most
　　Of what short time he had;
He praised the beauties of the Isle
　　At sunset's gentle hour,
And how the scene was more enhanced
　　Beneath its witching power.

He talked about the Lunar Bow,—
　　A th.ng he'd never seen,—
For when he strove to gain a point,
　　No bar could come between.
Still, as he talked his heart was moved,
　　More eloquent he grew,
And pictures, soft with lunar light,
　　With master hand he drew.

So sweet a picture he did paint,
　　She spoke with accents warm,
"Oh, how delighted I should be
　　Could I but own the charm!
But Aunt and Uncle, both, you see,
　　Are growing rather old,
And fear that in the evening air
　　They might perchance take cold."

"And having no acquaintance here,
    A stranger, I might say,
I cannot view this lovely place
    Except by light of day.
I know it must be lovely, and
    I very fain would see,
But fear my wishes are in vain,
    And that it cannot be."

Here was a chance, the which friend John
    Did instantly improve,
Yet tried to hold his eagerness
    In check, so he might move
Her to accept that which he now
    Unto her did propose,
Yet feared the while, that she in him,
    Might not full faith repose.

He kindly offered to escort
    Her round the Isle that eve,
And boldly said that if she chose
    He'd ask her Uncle's leave;
But this she rather feared, and said
    'Twould be as well, if he
Would meet her where they met at first,
    And thus they did agree.

So here our Hero did repair
  As in the first I said,
And silent watched, and waited for
  The coming of the maid;
An hour at least had come and gone,
  Yet not to him it brought
The bright fulfillment of his dream,
  The maiden whom he sought.

And this, the trouble was, of which
  I in the first place spoke,
And tho' he watched and waited long,
  No step the silence broke;
No step? Oh, yes! there plenty were,
  But they no form revealed
Unto his waiting, weary heart,
  Which o'er him power did wield.

Well, tired of walking, he at length
  Upon a stone sat down,
The look expectant on his face
  Soon changed into a frown.
He called himself a precious fool,
  And some such other name
Which people angry with themselves
  Occasionally claim.

"Confound that girl! why her I swear
  I've fooled away the eve,
When well I knew to—morrow morn
  I shall be forced to leave;
Hang all the women any way!
  They never keep their word;
They prate of being true till death,
  Was e'er such nonsense heard?"

But here his conscience gave a twinge,
  As mem'ry brought to mind
The features of a country lass
  Whom he had left behind;
And, as he thought of how for years
  She'd ever proved but true,
His deeds of wilful faithlessness
  Seemed passing in review.

" Ah, Betsy Jane! dear Betsy Jane!
  I've faithless been I know,
I'm sure if *you* had made the trip
  You'd never served me so;
I well remind the eve I left
  We lingered at the bars,
And plighted o'er again our troth,
  Beneath the twinkling stars."

"I promised faithful to be true,
    In fact, I think I swore
That thy sweet image in my heart
    Should live forevermore;
And that no form however fair,
    Should for a moment hold
The heart of him whose fate henceforth
    Should be by thee controlled."

"Such promises are easy made,
    And should be kept I know,
But ev'ry heart, I fear, sometimes,
    Is prone to wand'ring go.
I know that such has been the case
    With me, since I left home,
In proof of which I merely ask,
    Why don't that maiden come?"

"By jingo! every body's in,
    And doubtless gone to bed,
I guess I'll follow up the plan,
    And take the way they've led.
I'll take the train to-morrow morn,
    And back, I swear I'll go!
And all this foolish fancy, I
    Unto the winds will throw."

Thus spoke our hero, but, alas!
　I mourn indeed for him,
His chance that night for peaceful rest
　To tell the truth was slim;
He strove full hard to go to sleep,
　Yet lay awake to think,
And in the morning rose to feel
　He hadn't slept a wink.

He missed the cars, but didn't care,
　'Twould give him one chance more,
He stared at every one he met
　And watched each Hotel door.
He watched indeed, but watched in vain
　To gain of her a sight,
He wished some one would hit him, so
　He'd have a cause to fight.

He fooled around at such a rate
　The last train it had gone,
Then woke to realize, that yet
　His visit was undone;
So, as he'd nothing else to do,
　He thought an hour he'd while
Away, by going o'er to see
　The sun set from the Isle.

The Poets boast of beauteous skies
  In fair Italia's clime,
And chant their praise of sunset scenes
  In mellow tinted rhyme,
In fancy 'mong Venetian hills
  Their wand'ring steps they bend,
Where Adriatic wave and sky,
  In bright alembic blend.

That skies of Italy are fair,
  'Tis folly to refute,
But that they fairer are than mine
  I ever shall dispute.
The sunset hour of every clime
  Hath beauties of its own,
But fairer than Columbia's skies,
  I claim that there are none.

And, if a native of the soil,
  Would boast a scene to match,
Come! let him stand beside me here,
  And from the Island watch
Upon a sea of Amethyst
  With amber waves upcurled.
The fleecy cloud-ships of the west
  With golden sails unfurled!

Then, let him say, if that he can,
  Or that his truth be flown,
The boasted skies of Italy
  Are fairer than his own;
E'en as I write, I bow beneath
  The glory of that power,
Sent by our God to soothe the heart
  At sunset's holy hour.

Low sinks the sun adown the west
  Through purple mist and gold,
Which like the curtains of a couch
  Lie lightly fold on fold;
And, as the sun sinks from my view
  Beyond yon hills afar,
"Night draws her sable curtain round
  And pins it with a star."

Here, where the river's endless flood,
  Rolls down in ceaseless flow,
I stood with thee, oh; joyous thought!
  One little year ago.
Here saw the sun in glory die,
  Here saw him sink to rest,
Here felt the pressure of thy lips
  And held thee to my breast.

Oh, glorious eve ! to memory dear,
  Thy mystic witching power,
Shall thrill my soul as oft as time
  May bring the sunset hour;
No scene to come, no time, no change,
  Can take thee from my mind,
But in my heart each burning word
  Shall fondly be enshrined.

But how with thee ? oh, precious one
  Who stood beside me here !
Shall I within thy mem'ry live,
  And still to thee be dear ?
Or when the years swift rolling on
  Shall bear us down life's tide,
Wilt thou forget the one who watched
  The sunset by thy side ?

Oh, tell me not if this be so !
  Still let me fondly dream
That in thy heart I'll henceforth live,
  And ever to thee seem
As dear as when we, side by side,
  Felt that fond witching power,
Which henceforth all my life shall thrill
  When comes the sunset hour.

But there! I guess I've done it now,
  That last confounded strain
Has turned me topsy-turvy, and,
  Has quite upset my brain.
But John, I'm very glad to say
  Some common sense yet had,
And viewed the scene like common folks,
  Nor got with rapture mad.

But may be, it was on account
  Of what he'd just gone through,
That John could not appreciate
  The glory of the view.
Although, perchance, in after years,
  He'll think this tale a myth,
And maybe quite forget that e'er
  He met with sweet Miss Smith.

But now, I guess 'tis time for me
  To bid our John farewell,
He's made some blunders on his trip
  Which I have tried to tell.
But I've made blunders too, as well,
  I'll say so since you know it,
In fact, with John and I, 'tis just
  Such Hero, and such Poet.

Now, if I followed up the plan
   Of writers of the day,
To some fair maid whom he has met
   I'd give our John away.
But, as I'm not sensational,
   Nor of my Hero vain,
I guess I'll send him home, and let
   Him marry Betsy Jane.

THE END.

www.ingramcontent.com/pod-product-compliance
Lightning Source LLC
Chambersburg PA
CBHW020027030726
47499CB00007B/2306